RYDER AND PIPER THE PUPPY

For Ophelia,

Reading is a gift.

Enjoy!

TAILS FROM SOUTHERN SEASONS FARM
Book 1

RYDER AND
PIPER THE PUPPY

author
KATHY DUFFY

illustrator
JEDD KAHN

LANIER PRESS

DEDICATION

The Feral Cat Program of Georgia,
the rescue group Sienna was rescued from.

Georgia Equine Rescue League,
the rescue group Darling was rescued from.

And to all of the people who open their homes to
foster and restore the health of animals in need.
Thank you.

LANIER
PRESS an Imprint of
BookLogix
Alpharetta, GA

ISBN: 978-1-6653-0263-0 - Paperback
eISBN: 978-1-6653-0264-7 - eBook

Library of Congress Control Number: 2021916596

Printed in the United States of America   0 8 2 5 2 1

∞ This paper meets the requirements of ANSI/NISO Z39.48-1992
(Permanence of Paper)

Illustrations by Fedd Kahn

CONTENTS

Family Photo

It was Christmas Eve, and Ryder—a purebred Miniature Australian Shepherd—was happy. The nub of his tail wagged with excitement, and his eyes brightened with anticipation at the red, white, and green twinkling lights on the evergreen tree. Shiny ornaments in different shapes and sizes dotted the tree from top to bottom.

One particular ornament stood out from all the others. It was supposed to look like Ryder, but it looked more like a reindeer than a dog. He barked at it, trying to tell his family that the dangling, shiny object wasn't him. But all they did was smile and pet him. For whatever reason, animals understood everything humans said, but humans couldn't comprehend anything an animal said.

During his five years of his life, Ryder realized that people had many traditions. For the most part, he liked them because they meant family time, and he loved being with his human family. The only tradition he didn't like was wearing matching pajamas on Christmas Eve for the holiday family photo. If it were possible, he'd tell his family that clothing felt strange over his long, fluffy red and white fur.

Ryder lived on a hobby farm called Southern Seasons Farm, where horses, goats, cats, chickens, and bees roamed freely.

Ryder was shy around people and didn't like anyone touching him that wasn't a member of his family. He was also somewhat shy when it came to other animals. And even though he'd started training at an early age and had been a star student in every class, it still didn't help overcome his shyness. But he did have a special bond with his Mom because she stayed home with him while Dad went to work in an office.

The only other animal on the farm that Ryder felt comfortable with was Sienna, an eight-year-old Siamese cat rescued by Mom when she was one day old.

Sienna was bottle-fed and hand-raised by Mom. They bonded quickly, and the cat grew up believing she was a human too.

Ryder often told Sienna that she was a sophisticated feline with beautiful features—like her cream and chocolate-colored fur and vivid blue eyes. But, she'd always turn a deaf ear and proudly stroll away with her head held high.

Now, as Ryder continued to stare at the Christmas tree, he didn't hear Sienna when she came into the living room.

"Are you wondering what you'll get for Christmas?" she asked, sitting beside him. She didn't give Ryder a chance to answer before she added, "I'm excited about all the wrapping paper, bows and strings the family will throw on the floor. It's so much fun to slide on the paper and toss the bows in the air. I can't wait!"

"You're such a cat," Ryder said, holding back a chuckle.

"I beg your pardon; I'm not a cat!" responded Sienna with a tone of superiority. "I'm a lady who knows how to have a good time."

Ryder rolled his eyes. "Sienna, stop and think about this: If you're a human, you'd be wearing matching pajamas for our Christmas Eve photo—like the rest of the family."

"It's not my fault Mother can't find my size," said Sienna. "And I cringe at the thought of those four-legged onesies."

Ryder knew better than to argue with a stubborn cat. Trying to convince her that she was a cat was like trying to convince the sky it was the ground.

He changed the subject. "Do you think the family will give me a bone or a ball for Christmas this year?" His stubby tail wagged double time.

"Well, Ryder, I happen to know what the family got for you, and I want you to promise that you'll be patient and open-minded tomorrow morning." She strolled off to sit by the fireplace for the holiday photo with the family.

"What do you mean?" asked Ryder, taking his place next to her.

Sienna ignored the question and posed regally for the camera.

The Gift

"It's Christmas Day, Ryder, and everything is so wonderful!" exclaimed Sienna amidst a bevy of ribbons and festive holiday paper on the floor. She happily flicked at a shiny green bow that sailed through the air.

"Everybody is so happy," said Ryder. "And the kitchen has some unusually good smells coming out of it. Mom said I'd be getting my gift next." Ryder spun excitedly in circles.

Sienna reminded him to be patient and open-minded.

Just then, Mom and Dad came into the room. Mom was cradling something small in her arms, and it moved.

"Merry Christmas, Ryder," said Mom. "This is your new little sister, Piper the Puppy."

Piper, rescued from an animal shelter, was a mixed breed; part Australian Shepherd, Australian Cattle Dog, Chocolate Labrador, Golden Retriever, and several other things. She was a super mutt, with the red color of an Australian Shepherd and the head and ears of a Labrador. When she wagged her long tail, it went in a circle instead of going side to side like most dogs. She was eight weeks old and weighed only three pounds. But because of her huge personality, she felt like a full-grown dog.

Mom placed Piper on the floor several feet in front of Ryder and stepped back.

Ryder also stepped back. "Wait, WHAT? I wanted a new ball! I don't want or need a little sister!" His words were clear and strong, but only Sienna and Piper heard him.

"I told you to please be patient and open minded," said Sienna, lowering her voice as if everyone in the room could hear her.

"Why, oh why, couldn't they just this once understand me?" asked Ryder. "A puppy is loud and, anyway, I like my privacy and alone time. How could I do that with a pesky little sister buzzing around all the time? What if she messes with my things and wants to sleep in my bed? Or, worse yet, tries to eat my food!"

Neither Ryder nor Sienna noticed that Piper was cowering under the coffee table. All the attention, the new house, smells, Ryder's remarks, and Sienna's strange face made the puppy quiver with fear.

"It's okay, Piper," said Sienna. "This is your new home, and we're happy you're here. Right, Ryder?"

"Yeah, sure. But…." Ryder paused when he caught a glimpse of Sienna's warning eyes.

"Hel-lo," said Piper in a shaky voice. She crawled out from under the table and sat up. And then, out of nowhere came a barrage of questions. "So, you're going to be my big brother? What are you going to teach me? What do you like to play? What's your favorite game? Do you like to play chase? I like to play chase; it's my favorite. Do you want to chase me, or do you want me to chase you? Will you teach me how to catch a ball? Can I sleep with you at night? Where are all of our toys?"

Piper never took a breath or waited for any answers. Instead, she started running round and round, jumping, and touching everything. The puppy's energy level was overwhelming for both Sienna and Ryder.

Sienna picked up a piece of red ribbon and strolled away.

Ryder went after her. "Where are you going?"

"I'm going to my favorite hiding place," she replied. "Piper is your present; not mine."

It didn't take Ryder long to find that his new sister was loud, constantly on the move, and didn't have a shy bone in her body. She wanted everyone to be her friend, especially her new big brother.

Piper ambled over to Ryder and jumped on top of him.

Ryder scrambled to his feet and rushed away. "Do not touch me!" he warned.

"I want to play!" exclaimed Piper happily.

"It's okay to play, but please don't jump on me," said Ryder with a scowl. "Have you ever heard of personal space?"

"Is personal space the first thing you are going to teach me, big brother?" asked Piper.

"Why, yes, it is," responded Ryder, knowing he'd just outsmarted the little pup.

For the next two weeks, every time Piper tried to get close to Ryder, he'd growl, letting her know she was in his personal space. It didn't bother Piper in the slightest, as she was enjoying her new life.

Ryder soon realized that his quiet household might never be peaceful again. He also realized there were many differences in his and Piper's personalities. Where he liked peace, she liked chaos. Where he didn't like strangers, she liked everyone. Where he liked to sit and learn, Piper was out exploring.

Ryder kept to himself, but watching Piper in those weeks did give him a few good chuckles. She was petite and physically unable to do the things a full-grown dog could do. But that didn't stop her from trying.

Everything Ryder did, Piper followed and imitated—like the time Ryder leaped onto the sofa to take a nap, and Piper tried to follow him up. She struggled for ten minutes to jump, climb, and figure out a way to reach the cushions, but her puppy legs were too short and not strong enough. She finally wore herself out and fell asleep on the floor by the couch. It was apparent she didn't want to be far from her big brother. She wanted him to accept her.

While Ryder did admire the puppy's determination, he was also grateful to have the couch to himself.

Then there was the time when Piper decided it would be fun to play tug of war with Sienna's tail. Appalled that the puppy would dare to put any part of her anatomy in her mouth, Sienna swatted her on the nose, "Release me, you tyrant!" Sienna yelled.

Oh, yes, Ryder found that especially funny.

One day, Piper sat across from Ryder and said, "I'm almost ten weeks old. I can obey commands—like *sit*, *down*, and *come* because you're a great teacher. Are you proud of me?" she asked, hoping that Ryder would give her praise.

"Yes," responded Ryder. "You've been working hard and have proven yourself to be a smart puppy. But, there's so much more for you to learn."

Piper's tail wagged so fast and hard that Ryder was sure she'd take off like a helicopter.

"We're going to be the best siblings ever!" exclaimed Piper.

"I agree," said Ryder with a sincere smile on his face. "Even though we're different, we'll find ways to compromise. We don't have to be the same to like one another. And I'm sure we'll have many exciting adventures too."

Wind Shadow

A few weeks later it was outdoor playtime, and Ryder and Piper were going to enjoy every minute of it.

Ryder wasn't bothered by the cold, blustery wind that whipped through the fenced-in pasture at the rear of his family's farmhouse. His topcoat of flowy fur had a downy undercoat that kept him warm.

Piper wasn't so lucky. Her thin coat of fur offered no protection from wintry weather. It was the puppy's endless running and jumping that made her feel warm.

The bright afternoon sun beamed down through the barren branches of the old chestnut tree at the side of a white gazebo. The tree had dropped its spiky pods. Inside the pods were prized chestnuts that squirrels collected and stored for the winter months.

Ryder and Piper loved to chase squirrels and other farm animals too. And today was no different.

While chasing the squirrels, Ryder and Piper bumped into Darling, a black Shetland pony mare with a long, thick flowing mane and tail.

Before coming to the farm, the pony—a neglected animal saved by a local rescue group—was in desperate need of medical attention. Once she was healthy, Southern Seasons Farm became her forever home. That's when Mom decided that the perfect name for such a darling creature had to be *Darling*.

When the pony came to live on the farm, two other horses—Dreamy and Charming—immediately fell in love with her. She was, after all, loveable and sweet. Though it wasn't Darling's nature to be fearful, she was cautious. Because of her past, she was still learning to trust people.

Things that frightened her, such as fly spray or having a winter blanket put on, took a lot of patience. But, she did her best to believe in her new parents and surroundings.

Soon, Darling learned to love every human that came to visit. Now she lived each day to the fullest.

A stall was built for her small stature with a gate rather than a wooden sliding door. There was a window lower to the ground so she could easily see out. She had a perfect view of everything that happened inside the barn. She often spent her days with the other horses and two goats named Foxy and Shandy.

Today, there was only Darling, Ryder, and Piper in the pasture.

When Piper spotted Darling, she dashed over to her and yelled, "Let's play pretend!"

"I don't want to play," said Darling. "I just want to graze on the sweet tuffs of grass before its time to go inside my stall for the night."

"Oh, come on," Piper begged. She turned to Ryder and said, "Tell her to play with us."

Ryder sighed heavily. "Darling, if you don't

play, Piper will make you the villain of the game anyway."

"Then, I'm the villain," answered Darling.

Piper darted into the gazebo. "I'm Princess Piper; and this is my castle!" she shouted. "The Wind Shadow and her evil minions are after me. If they catch me, I'll surely be doomed!"

Ryder knew better than to protest. He was up for a good game, so he played along. "I'll be the King of Canines, and I shall save you, Princess Piper," he said gallantly. "Listen! I hear the Wind Shadow, and she's sending her minions now. Run for your life!"

A gust of wind blew, and the branches of the chestnut tree swayed, hurling long, spooky shadows across the ground.

"Watch out!" yelled Ryder. "Those monstrous arms are trying to capture us!"

They dashed out to the pasture and ran around twice to the left and three times to the right, not stopping until they were safely back inside the gazebo.

"For now," Piper said breathlessly, "we're safe from the evil clutches of the Wind Shadow."

Ryder, standing tall, looked every bit like a king. "Do not worry, Princess," he said. "I have devised a plan to chase the minions away."

"How, King Ryder?" asked Piper.

Ryder pointed to the chestnut tree. "There they are!" he said quietly, not wanting to alert the minions.

As soon as Piper saw two harmless bushy tail squirrels resting on a branch, she began to tremble. "I—I see them," she replied in a shaky voice.

"Those are the Wind Shadow's minions," explained Ryder. "We must chase them away, so they can no longer torture us.

Piper spotted Darling and called out to her: "Wind Shadow, you may control the wind and shadows, but you're about to lose all of your powers. We're going to take your little minions!"

In a flash, Piper and Ryder ran toward the tree, barking and jumping against its trunk. Knowing they were safe from the annoying dogs, the squirrels climbed higher into the tree and disappeared. Ryder and Piper convinced themselves that the minions had been defeated.

"We are victorious!" Piper cheered.

"We are indeed!" announced Ryder. "I have saved the kingdom and Princess Piper."

Darling watched in amazement at how much energy Ryder and Piper used. Their behavior made no sense. That's when she decided to end the game and play the villain.

Rocking back on her haunches, she started galloping toward them. At that very moment, a bright beam of sunlight shone down over her lustrous black coat, making her look menacing. A gust of wind ruffled her mane, and her tail lifted high as she chased the two dogs into the gazebo.

"I am the Wind Shadow!" exclaimed Darling. "And you will never defeat me! I am speed and wind, mighty and powerful! Neither Princess Piper nor the King of Canines can tame the Wind Shadow!"

Piper and Ryder stared in awe.

Darling continued, rearing up on her two hind legs as her front legs reached high into the air. "You may have defeated my minions for now, but they will return! No one can stop the Wind Shadow!" She roared like a true villain.

"Wow!" exclaimed Ryder.

"Darling, you're the best villain in the entire world," Piper said, wagging her tail.

"Thank you very much," Darling said, bowing her head.

Just then, Mom called both dogs to come inside for dinner.

As Ryder headed for the house, he looked back at Darling. He remembered the day when she'd come to live on the farm and how weak her spirit was. Now, shining in all her glory, she had come full circle.

Game aside, there was no doubt that Darling was the winner. She was living a real fairytale and would have her happily ever after.

How Now Brown Cow

Three months had passed, and the first leaves and flowers of spring were blooming. Early spring was also the time that calves were born.

Ryder and Piper barked loudly, signaling Mom that they were ready to go for their morning walk. As soon as Mom put their leashes on, they tugged excitedly, knowing there was a newborn calf on one of the neighboring farms.

Before long, they spotted the baby cow standing alone at the fence line.

"Hey, little brown cow," called Piper. "Do you know that your daddy is royalty? He's Sir Loin." The puppy laughed heartily.

Ryder gave Piper a questioning stare that went unnoticed.

The little calf looked at Piper blankly.

Piper continued. "What do you call a cow that doesn't give milk? A milk dud! No, wait, an udder failure!" Piper now roared with laughter even though Ryder and the young calf remained silent.

Mom gave the leashes a gentle tug, and they continued walking.

Piper was still laughing as they headed home.

"How come you're not laughing, Ryder?" asked Piper.

Ryder glared at the puppy. "I can't take you any-where," he said in a tone of disappointment.

"What does that mean?" asked Piper.

"It means I'm embarrassed by your behavior," replied Ryder. "On days like today, I'm glad Mom doesn't understand our words."

Piper rolled her amber eyes. "Don't you know how to take a joke?" she asked.

"There's a fine line between joking and bully-ing," said Ryder.

Piper chuckled. "Bullying? Oh, I get it; he's a baby bull. Good one, Ryder."

"That's not what bullying means," said Ryder. "If you're telling a joke, you should be sure it's not at another animal's expense, or they might think you're laughing at them. There's a big difference between having fun and making fun of him or her. I'm not sure if the young calf understood your re-marks. And, in that case, what you did is called bullying."

"Oh, come on, Ryder, I'm sure he thought it was funny. They were only jokes," Piper replied.

"Did he laugh or smile even a little?" Ryder asked.

The expression on Piper's face changed. "Well, no, but—"

"There are no buts," interrupted Ryder. "You embarrassed me today, and I'm ashamed of your behavior."

Determined to have the last word, Piper said, "Whatever."

The rest of the day and the following morning the two dogs did not talk or play with one another. Ryder knew that Piper still had some growing up to do. But the puppy didn't see it that way. She wanted to have fun with her brother, so she decided to break the silence.

"Are you looking forward to our walk today, Ryder?" asked Piper nervously.

"I'm not going," Ryder said matter-of-factly.

"If Mom says you're going, then you have to."

Piper shot back as if Ryder wasn't aware that Mom was the boss, not him.

"Mom may not understand our words, but she certainly understands our body language," said Ryder. "She won't make me go, and I will not go for anymore walks with a bully like you."

Ryder was finished with the conversation and left Piper standing alone to think about what he'd said.

When Mom called them to go for a walk, Ryder tucked his tail and slinked away from the front door. Just as he'd predicted, Mom grabbed one leash. "It's just you and me, Piper," she said, and off they went.

Piper considered the possibility that Ryder could be right about bullying. What if she did hurt the young animal's feelings?

As they approached the cow farm, Piper saw the young calf. She was embarrassed and nervous but knew what she had to do.

"Hi, remember me?" she asked the calf timidly.

The calf stared but didn't respond.

Piper moved closer to the fence. "I'm really

sorry if I hurt your feelings yesterday. I didn't mean to. I like jokes and was just trying to have fun and make you laugh."

The calf lifted his head. And suddenly, in a high-pitched voice, he said, "Knock knock."

Piper was pleasantly surprised. "Who's there?" she asked quickly.

"Get along," replied the calf.

"Get along who?" asked Piper.

"Get along little doggie!" And now, it was the calf's turn to laugh hysterically.

Piper wagged her tail and said, "That's a good one."

"My name is Mookie," said the calf. "Thanks for the apology."

From that moment, Piper and Mookie became good friends.

Piper was happy but knew she had to make things right with Ryder.

As soon as she returned home, she dashed into the den and saw Ryder and Sienna sitting on the couch, talking. It looked as if they were having a serious discussion.

"Excuse me, Ryder," Piper said softly.

Ryder looked down and gave the puppy a nod.

"I apologized to the calf for my behavior yesterday, and he forgave me. His name is Mookie, and we're going to be good friends. He likes jokes too. I'm sorry if I embarrassed you. I hope you forgive me."

Ryder jumped off the couch and gave Piper a high five with his paw.

Piper returned the gesture.

Sienna jumped off the couch. "What's it called when the treats are gone?" she asked.

Ryder and Piper widened their eyes and shrugged.

"Oh, you silly dogs. It's a cat-tastrophe! Get it?"

The house filled with laughter, but only the animals understood the joke.

Friend or Foe

Piper was growing up, and her training increased. There were days when she liked learning, and then there were times when she just wanted to do her own thing. And that meant running and playing with Ryder and the other animals on the farm. But the first thing on her daily to-do list was simple: be happy and make others laugh.

Occasionally, when Ryder didn't want to be bothered, Piper would pester Sienna. But that always depended on the cat's mood. If Sienna refused to play, Piper would nip at her. And, as everyone on the farm knew, Sienna disliked any part of her body to be touched.

What others failed to realize was that Piper was still teething. Everything went straight into her mouth and was chewed, regardless of who or what it was.

It was mid-morning when Piper finished her obedience lessons. She dashed out to the screened-in porch and saw Ryder and Sienna basking in the sun.

"Let's play!" squealed Piper, jumping up and down.

"Not now," Ryder said with a yawn.

Piper turned her attention to Sienna and, with pleading eyes, asked her to play.

Sienna directed her gaze to the garden. "Not now," she said, dismissing Piper. "I'm busy watching the birds and squirrels."

Piper grinned and Sienna could see the holes from her missing puppy teeth.

"Are you going to try and chew on me?" Sienna asked nervously. "I'm not a chew toy! And, furthermore, we ladies don't like to get our hair messed up."

"I'll try not to do that," replied Piper with a sneaky grin. "But I can't make any promises."

"Well, in that case, I will not play with you," said Sienna. "I refuse to walk around looking gross from dog slobber. Yuck! Just the thought of smelling like a wet dog sickens me."

Ryder heard Piper and Sienna's conversation. He stayed silent, hoping the two would play together so he could enjoy his nap. But Sienna's last comment insulted him as much as it did the little pup.

Ryder suddenly felt the urge to speak up. "Sienna, dog slobber is no worse than cat drool."

"Humph, I wouldn't know since I'm a human and not a cat!" she exclaimed.

"Here we go again," said Ryder. "If you're a human, you wouldn't be able to understand me or Piper or any other animal."

Sienna was quick with a comeback. "I guess I must be special, just like Mother tells me. I've had enough of you canines; I'm going to my hiding spot."

"We all know your hiding spot is in Mom's closet!" exclaimed Piper.

Sienna held her head high and strolled away. "Yes, and there are no animals allowed in there!"

"Evidently cats are!" Ryder answered sharply.

He and Piper tried to muffle their boisterous laughter, but it was impossible. So, to cover up their loud behavior, they started a game of chase—running round and round the couch and the coffee table.

When Piper took off into the kitchen, Ryder chased her around the counter where Mom was preparing lunch for her book club friends. Just then the doorbell rang, as soon as Mom opened the door to welcome her friends Ryder started barking as the visitors tried to touch him and Piper began jumping on them. Disappointed in the dog's behavior, Mom took them to the bedroom, gave them a stern look and locked them inside.

"You see what you did!" cried Ryder.

"It's not my fault you're so loud," said Piper.

Sienna came out of her closet. "What are you two arguing about now?" she inquired.

Piper was quick to respond. "We got locked in the bedroom because Mom's having friends over, and Ryder's too shy to let them touch him so he barked."

Ryder quickly retaliated. "That's not true! Piper jumps all over the visitors. That's why we're stuck in here."

Sienna remained quiet, hoping they'd find a way to settle their latest argument. Most of the time, they got along—except when their personalities got in the way. And this was one of those times.

"Perhaps I can settle this," Sienna finally said. "You both bring out the best and the worst of each other. Did it occur to either one of you that you're locked in here because of loud barking and non-stop jumping? I don't imagine Mother approves of this type of behavior in our home."

The thought of Mom not being proud of him immediately humbled Ryder.

Piper, however, found Sienna's remark confusing. She saw her jumping as playful and a sign that she liked people and animals.

Ryder and Piper remained silent, knowing they were equally responsible for being locked away.

"I think you owe one another an apology," said Sienna.

"I'm sorry," said Ryder.

"Sorry," chimed Piper.

"And you both owe me an apology, too," declared Sienna. "You invaded my space with your loudness. I was peaceful in my closet until the two of you came along."

"Sienna is right," said Piper. "Ryder, if you don't like strangers you should stay away from them."

"Well, Piper, if you want to play with every stranger you meet, do it respectfully with all four feet on the ground," replied Ryder. "Sienna, I'm sorry if I bothered you, but I can't stay here. It's my job to be with Mom and make sure she's safe."

"As long as you are afraid of strangers, you can't protect Mother or anyone else," said Sienna.

"I'm not scared of people," replied Ryder. "I just don't see why I have to be close to them. I have the two of you, the other animals on the farm, and the family. That's all I need."

"Not me!" Piper declared. "The more the merrier. I want to be friends with everybody! I want to play ball and fetch a stick. And I wouldn't mind if someone wanted to pet me or put out their hand to high five my paw."

Sienna, being the voice of reason, said, "Piper it's great to have friends and meet new people, but you have to be respectful. And you also have to listen to Mother when it comes to meeting strangers. In a perfect world it may appear that people and animals have good intentions, but the world is not perfect; we need to be careful."

"That's good advice," said Piper. "But, as we all know, I'm Piper the Puppy and everybody loves me!"

Lessons in the Park

Early the next day, Ryder and Piper went to puppy training with Mom at the doggie park. They went once a week and met the same group of people and puppies for lessons. Mom took Ryder so he'd have more exposure to strangers. The trainer was happy to use him as an example of how command and obedience worked together.

Ryder knew how to behave and liked it when the trainer called him a good boy. What he didn't like was when Mom allowed a stranger to give him a treat. And although he only wanted treats from Mom, he did understand why she was doing it.

Piper was the exact opposite of her big brother. She wanted to play with the other puppies and run free. So, when she noticed a man and his dog playing ball, her first thought was to join them. After all, chasing balls was one of her favorite games.

The man's dog was fast and could jump super high to catch the ball. Piper wondered if she could jump that high too. She wanted to break free from Mom and find out.

Halfway through her lesson, Piper got her chance. As soon as she saw the man raise his arm to throw the ball, she took off, zigzagging her way toward him. When she jumped to catch it, the man shouted, "NO! BAD DOG!"

From across the park, Mom yelled, "Piper, come!"

Piper didn't obey, and the man's dog snarled and snapped at her, biting her shoulder.

When Piper realized that the man and his dog didn't want to play or be her friend, she yelped and backed away with her tail between her hind legs.

Mom, with Ryder on his leash, came running over. From the look on Piper's face, both Mom and Ryder knew she was scared. Her pride hurt more than the scratch.

When they arrived home, Ryder explained to Sienna what had taken place at the park.

In her defense, Piper said that the man called her a bad dog when it was *his* dog that bit her.

"Piper, I told you to be careful of strangers," said Sienna. "More importantly, if you had listened to Mother and trusted her when she gave you the command to come, you wouldn't have been hurt. Right?"

"Yes, I guess so," said Piper. "I just thought everybody liked to play. That's what we do when we go to the park."

"You should know better by now," said Ryder. "Look at me. I'm almost six years old, and I still don't trust strangers. It's who I am, and not everybody wants to play all the time."

"We all have different ways, and that's okay," said Sienna. "Can you imagine how boring life would be if we were all the same. We need to accept and respect each other. We can be different and still enjoy each others company." Sienna hoped the puppy had learned a life lesson she'd never have to learn again.

"From now on, I'm going to listen to Mom and work harder on my commands at puppy training," said Piper. "That way I can have more playtime with my classmates. They're all nice, and we get along. None of them have ever been mean to me, and their parents have never called me a bad dog."

"Good idea, Piper," said Ryder. "Plus, you never know when Mom will invite one of your friends over for a puppy play date. Not all animals are as lucky as we are to live on a farm and have large pastures to play in. And, as we know, Mom loves animals and wants to give them the opportunity to run free and play."

"I would love to have friends over," said Piper. "we would run until we were exhausted!"

"I think we've learned an important lesson today," said Ryder. "But, just so you know, when you have friends over, I'll probably stay inside and read a book."

Piper laughed. "How about you, Sienna?"

"I'm with Ryder. You and your friends can do puppy things; I'm going to stay inside where it's quiet."

"That's a deal," said Piper. "I know you both enjoy and need your own space and quiet time. When you want, we can all play together."

Sienna smiled. "You know what, Piper the Puppy? You're going to be a fine dog one day."

The compliment made Piper happy. She wagged her tail, knowing that Sienna would always be her forever friend.

A Book for Everyone

One rainy morning, Piper found herself with nothing to do. Sienna was in her closet, and Ryder was reading a book. She didn't like it when Ryder read books because it meant he'd be occupied and not play with her.

"Wow, Ryder, you have a lot of books!" exclaimed Piper. "Have you read all of them?"

"Ten, to be exact. I'm trying to decide which one I want to read next." Ryder answered.

"I don't like to read. It's boring." Piper said.

"Then you haven't read the right book," said Ryder.

"What do you mean, the *right* book?" asked Piper.

Ryder explained. "There are different kinds of books: humor, educational, books about faraway lands, fantasy, and so much more. If you can imagine it, there's a book about it. You need to read a book that will interest *you*."

"What's your favorite book? I'll try that one

because if you like it then I'll like it too." Piper declared.

"It doesn't work that way," Ryder responded. "Books are as different to the reader as personalities. I like to read poetry and history books that teach me about the past. You, on the other hand, are always on the go, so you'd probably enjoy action and adventure books."

"Yes!" Piper exclaimed excitedly. "Action sounds like fun. Do you have one of those?"

"As a matter of fact I do," Ryder said with a smile. He handed Piper a book.

"Do I have to read it all today? If I do, then I don't want to read."

"You can read at your own pace," said Ryder. "But once you start reading an interesting story, you won't want to stop until you've reached the end."

Piper didn't believe him, but she took the book anyway. She looked at the cover, and her eyes brightened. "Hey! This book is about space travel. Someday, I'd like to travel to the moon and beyond."

"Now's your chance," said Ryder.

Piper didn't understand what Ryder meant but decided to give reading a try. She nestled into her comfy doggie bed and opened to the first chapter.

It didn't take long before she saw herself as an astronaut. She heard the roar of the engines and felt the pressure of being propelled into space. Every word and every page moved her swiftly through the cosmos, zooming past planets, stars, and galaxies.

When the spaceship slowed, a puffy sparkling pink sphere came into view. The planet had three circling moons, each in a different pink color, ranging from pale to bright fuchsia. It was an undiscovered planet called Confection.

As soon as the spaceship landed, the doors popped open, and a delightful sweet-smelling fragrance filled the air. It was like stepping inside a candy shop where everything was pink. There were rivers of gooey cherry syrup, clouds of squishy cotton candy, and mountains of strawberry cupcakes and icing.

Piper's imagination soared. She ate as much candy as she could, and it all tasted delicious.

When she felt her paws getting clogged in sticky sugar, she trudged into to the spaceship and rocketed off to the next planet.

The turn of a page brought her to a new astrological find called Glow Cuttlefish. Tiny, twinkling yellow lights dotted the edge of the darkened planet. The spaceship landed softly, and the door opened. There was no way of telling if the planet had mountains or plants, rocks or water.

Her first thought was that there was nothing to see so she should move ahead in the story. But, she was curious about the yellow dots and kept on reading.

And that's when an army of slimy creatures crawled along the ground with long tentacles. Their luminous colors shined brightly, changing from green to blue, brown to gray. The one thing they had in common was the dazzling color of their yellow eyes. They were tiny octopuses, but there was no water in sight.

The creatures were as small as Piper's paws. Weird gulping sounds hiccupped around them as they circled her. Some squished up her body, all the way to her eyes, mouth, and ears, peeking inside the openings. One of them stuck a tentacle inside her nose, which made her sneeze so loudly that the other creatures started tickling her. She giggled uncontrollably and rolled on the ground. It was time to get back to the spaceship before she died laughing. She jumped up, shook off the aliens, and ran into the ship.

In a flash, she zoomed to the planet of Upset Boulder, where some rocks were smooth and others jagged. As soon as she stepped out of the spaceship, she found herself upside down. The planet had no gravity. She tumbled over and over, hitting her head against the rocks. The more she tumbled, the more bumps and bruises she got. She twisted and turned until she made her way back into the ship, landing on her four paws.

Visiting these three planets had worn her out. She was ready to head back to Earth, which she knew was the best planet of all. The End.

Piper had started and finished the book; it was that good! Ryder was right; reading was fun, and she enjoyed the adventure this book took her on.

She ran into the den where Ryder was still reading his book. "Guess what?" she shouted. "I read the book you gave me. The entire book, and I liked it! It was about space and cotton candy and tickle aliens and bumping your head and coming home!"

Ryder smiled at his little sister. "I'm glad you gave reading a second chance. I knew you'd like it if you found the right book."

"Yes, and now I see why you like to read," said Piper. "I still want to run and play, but reading is not as terrible as I thought it would be."

"There's no reason why you can't do it all," said Ryder. "You pick the book, the time, and place you want to read. It's about having fun, and if you happen to learn something along the way, even better."

"I think books are going to bring a lot of exciting adventures into my life," said Piper. And, at that moment, she knew that someday she and her brother would have their own book club.

Learning the Hard Way

It was a hot summer day. The sun was shining brightly without a cloud to be seen. The temperature was high, and most of the animals on the farm were feeling the heat.

Ryder and Piper had found a shady spot next to the fence to lie down, trying not to overheat. When they looked across the pasture, they saw their friend, Shandy, a black Nubian goat, running up and down and all around. Her floppy brown ears bounced, making her look silly, which was fitting.

Shandy was a crossbreed from England, India, the Middle East, and North Africa. She wasn't bothered by the heat and acted as if it were just another day. The goat was an unusual soul; she not only liked the heat, but also spoke in rhyme.

Ryder had always admired Shandy because he felt her rhyming was a sign of intelligence. In all the years he had known her, he'd never heard her speak without rhyming.

Piper, however, was not a fan of poetry. Shandy's poems gave her a headache. In her mind, the goat talked too much—even if no one was listening or talking back.

Ryder kept an eye on Shandy. She was gazing at Mom's red rose bushes. Over the summer, the plants had grown, and the lush greenery spread through the fence.

When the goat started nibbling on the fragrant flowers, Ryder got up and warned her to stop. "I wouldn't do that if I were you. Mom will be mad if you eat her flowers."

Shandy swallowed the flower with one big gulp. "I like the flowers, which I shall devour. I'll eat the bush in less than an hour. Mom can be mad, and that's too bad. But this fine goaty will be oh so glad."

"Oh, geez, Ryder! Don't get her started," said Piper, as if Shandy couldn't hear. "It's too hot to put up with her rhymes. When she starts talking my head spins."

"Piper be nice," Ryder scolded.

Shandy took offense to Piper's comment and said, without missing a beat, "Little Piper, still in diapers, you run and screech so wildly hyper. If it weren't for Ryder, who has to chide her, she'd end up a stray alone to play."

"I would not be a stray!" exclaimed Piper indignantly. She pouted when realizing that she was the one that had started the fight.

Shandy laughed and trotted off. Not far off in the pasture was a wheelbarrow. So, she decided to make use of it because it looked like a boat. She jumped inside and loudly recited a poem, making sure that Piper and Ryder heard every word. "I am a goat with ears of brown, wearing a queen's coat and a beautiful crown. I will ride in my magical boat, until I reach my castle moat. For my home kingdom I will scour, where I will have my victory hour."

Piper raised her paws and covered her ears.

Shanty continued. "My enemies keep me hidden in a tower; they're just scandalous cads. But soon I'll regain my power, and they'll be sorry lads. When my feet hit the ground, my kingdom will be glad. My subjects will cheer, and take care of those scads!"

Shandy stepped out of the wheelbarrow and took a bow as if she'd given a royal performance.

Ryder clapped. "Bravo!"

Piper didn't clap. "Shandy!" she called, shaking her head. "You're so weird."

"Weird? I was just smeared," replied Shanty. "Your name calling is simply appalling. I have no reason not to conclude that Piper the Puppy is very rude."

Piper's brow ridge shot together. She had no defense since she was the one that called Shandy *weird*.

Just then, Mom headed toward the garden with a basket in her hand. She liked to pick fresh vegetables and herbs for the evening meal. Ryder and Piper wanted to be with her, so they trotted behind her.

The garden entrance had a gate to keep the farm animals away from the plants. Right in the middle of the garden was a shed that also served as a chicken coop. The enclosure had a wire roof and sides to keep the chickens protected from predators. Weeds pulled from the garden were given to the chickens as treats.

Ryder liked to sniff the different plants but had learned years ago not to eat anything unless it was offered to him. He had also known better than to mess with the chickens.

Piper, however, had not learned this lesson yet. She still liked to run around the chicken coop, which was annoying to the chickens. She couldn't get to them because of the wire, but it never stopped her from trying. Mom knew the chickens were safe, so she didn't mind if Piper wore herself out.

The chickens weren't amused, especially Avery, the rooster. So, when he saw Piper, he squawked loudly. "Go away you aggravating little dog!" he shouted. "You're annoying my hens!"

"Run, little dude, so I can chase you!" Piper shot back.

"I may be small, but I'm mighty, and you'd better watch it," said Avery. He puffed out his feathered chest. "I will protect my hens. Even Ryder knows that."

"Ryder's a mama's boy, and he's boring," Piper shot back.

Ryder and Avery made eye contact. Ryder's eyebrows shot up and Avery winked at him.

"Piper, do you want to hear a secret about Ryder?" Avery asked.

"Absolutely!" answered Piper.

"Come closer, and I'll tell you," said Avery.

Piper went to the fence and turned her ear to listen to the secret.

"Closer," said Avery.

Piper leaned in, and her ear touched the wire.

Instead of whispering, Avery reached through the fence with his sharp little beak and pecked at Piper's ear. The startled puppy barked.

Mom turned her attention to the chicken coop and told Piper to stop bothering the chickens.

Piper was confused. Avery was the one that bit *her*.

Ryder and Avery laughed.

Avery strutted away. "I told you I was small but mighty."

Piper lowered her tail and sat close to Ryder. She was pouting and looking for sympathy. "I don't know why I got in trouble when Avery is the one that hurt me."

"Piper, you started it," said Ryder. "You came into *their* yard and provoked them. Why do you think I don't chase the chickens? When I was a pup, Avery got me with his sharp little beak more than once. Now, we have an understanding, and I leave them alone, Avery doesn't peck at me, and Mom doesn't have to tell me to stop bothering them."

Piper had a hard time believing Ryder was ever a puppy and not a wise adult dog.

"Does Mom ever get mad at you?"

Ryder chuckled. "I'm not perfect, but I try to be the best dog I can be—even if you think that's being a mama's boy."

"You're always trying to please Mom. Sometimes I get jealous because I think you love her more than me."

Ryder licked Piper's hurt ear. "Not more, just differently. Mom rescued us, and now we have food, a home, and her love. It's in our breeding to care for humans. At the same time, you're my sister and even though we may drive each other nuts, I'll still love you unconditionally."

"Even if I'm your sister by adoption and not blood?" Piper asked.

"Of course," said Ryder. "I will love you, no matter what."

Piper sighed happily. "No matter what," she whispered.

Birthday Wishes

The end of October brought a change to the season with cool days and falling leaves that had turned to shades of gold, red, orange, and brown. Soon, the trees would be bare.

Every season on the farm was new and exciting for the animals, and especially for Piper. She'd grown from a three-pound pup to a whopping forty pounds. Even though her legs were long, which made her look like a gangly puppy, she was finally able to jump on the couch and lay beside her big brother.

Ryder, however, was not a happy dog. A

pestering sister was now able to invade his once quiet spot.

Sienna was lying on the floor, trying to catch the last of the afternoon light as it came through the window. The bright sun felt warm on her face, making her feel stress-free and happy. Above her, Ryder slept quietly. She shut her eyes and just before drifting off to sleep, Piper yelled, "Who wants to play a game of chase?"

Ryder opened one eye and turned over. "No, thanks," he said with a loud yawn.

"How about Duck Duck Goose?" asked Piper.

Sienna's eyes shot open. "What part of *no* don't you understand?" she asked.

Piper thought hard. "I got it! We'll play Cats and Dogs?"

Sienna knew Piper was trying to annoy her with the mention of cats. "Ryder and I don't want to play," she said firmly. "We're happy to be quiet; you should try it sometime." She got up and moved to the other side of the room.

Piper gave up on Sienna and looked at her

brother. She tapped her paw on his head. "Wake up, sleepy head," she said in a singsong voice.

"Please stop," Ryder said softly.

Piper stopped and started chewing on her brother's ear.

"Stop!" he said, raising his voice.

But this didn't stop Piper. So, she chewed on Ryder's tail and then his foot.

Ryder knew that Piper wasn't going to stop bothering him, so he jumped off the couch and decided to change the subject. "You know, Piper, today is your birthday," he said.

Piper wasted no time. She flew off the couch, and her tail wagged. "What's a birthday?" she asked curiously.

"Your first birthday is when you go from being a puppy to being a dog," explained Ryder. "You grow up and stop doing annoying things—like chewing on me or Sienna. You mature, nap more, and learn to control yourself."

Piper looked as if she'd tasted something sour. "I don't think I'm going to like birthdays," she declared.

"Birthdays are grand," said Sienna. "I've had several, but please don't ask how old I am; you never ask a lady her age."

Ryder held back a chuckle. "Piper, there are other benefits to being mature. One is that you can have as many naps as you'd like."

"Don't forget the birthday gifts," said Sienna. "And, of course, there'll be a special treat with a candle to blow out. That's when you make your birthday wish."

"A wish? What kind of wish?" Piper asked, suddenly intrigued.

"Anything you want," Sienna answered.

Piper paraded across the room. With a stylish flair, she turned and stood perfectly still, imaging cameras focused on her. "I'd like to become a famous runway model in Paris."

"That sounds exciting," said Sienna.

Piper continued. "All the fashion designers will ask for me—Piper the Puppy—to model their stylish clothes and fashionable collars. I'll be dripping in diamonds, emeralds, sapphires, and amber stones to match my eyes. And the best part will

be that all of the dogs from the Westminster Dog Show will want to date me!"

"I don't think Mom will allow you to date," said Sienna, holding back a chuckle.

Ryder didn't care what Piper wished for as long as it made her excited about becoming an adult dog.

Piper sat quietly. She had a faraway look in her eyes.

"Piper, what's on your mind?" asked Sienna.

"I'm going to change my wish. I want to be a veterinary nurse," she said. "I can help save lives and bring joy and laughter to as many animals as possible."

"What a wonderful wish," said Sienna. "Animals are often afraid, sad, and lonely when separated from their families."

"You're right!" exclaimed Piper. "When they're afraid, I can give them hugs. If they're nervous about shots, I'll tell them jokes to make them laugh and give them treats. By the time they leave, they'll be feeling better and know that Nurse Piper helped on their journey to healing."

Ryder and Sienna waited to see if Piper had another wish. She didn't disappoint them.

"I can be a firedog!" she said suddenly. "I'll be the one that rushes into burning buildings with the fire hose, spraying hundreds of gallons of water to put the fires out."

"I know you like to play in water," said Sienna. "I hate water."

"Me, too," said Ryder, heading toward the couch.

"Wait!" called Piper. "I have another wish!"

Ryder widened his eyes and waited.

"I want to be an equestrian!" Piper exclaimed. "I'll have my own horse and together we'll jump over high barriers and never knock over a single pole." Her tail wagged crazily as her imagination soared when she pictured herself with Olympian gold medals around her neck. "I can almost hear the accolades when I come into the riding arena on my mighty steed. My horse will dance and prance, showing off because he'll be proud to carry me on his back."

"Sounds wonderful," said Sienna.

"I think everybody will cheer for you," said Ryder.

"Yes! And I'll go down in history as the finest equestrian dog that ever lived."

"That's quite the wish," said Ryder. "On my first birthday, I wished to be the best I could be for Mom.

Piper laughed. "You know what your problem is, Ryder? You don't use your imagination enough."

Ryder didn't take offense to the remark. His only desire was to see Piper grow up and stop provoking him, Sienna, and the other animals. And, of course, stop putting everything in her mouth.

Meanwhile, Mom came into the den and gave Piper a new chew toy. She held a doggie bowl with a spoonful of peanut butter with a lit candle in its center.

Piper stood still as everybody sang Happy Birthday.

"Time to make your wish," said Sienna.

Piper took a deep breath and blew out the candle.

"Did you make a wish?" Ryder asked.

Piper paused and then grinned. "Yes, and it's the best wish of all! I wished to stay a puppy … FOREVER!"

Ryder covered his eyes with both paws and declared, "Piper, a puppy forever. I hope I survive!"

New Things to Come

A year had passed, and it was once again Christmas Eve. Mom was excited for the arrival of her two daughters to celebrate the holiday season. Pajamas for the annual holiday photo had been purchased, and everyone was looking forward to the festivities.

Ryder still didn't like or want to wear PJs. But Piper was excited, as this was going to be her first year in the family photo. Last year she didn't understand what the holiday meant, but now she had lots of questions.

Sienna and Ryder rested in the den where the Christmas tree stood in its usual spot.

Piper looked curiously at the holiday decorations. "Why is there a tree in here?" she asked.

"It's tradition," replied Ryder. "And our family puts gifts under the tree."

"Why are we going to take pictures in pajamas?" asked Piper.

"That's a tradition, too," said Sienna. "Mom puts all the photos in an album so that we can look at them every year and cherish the memories."

"Traditions are practices passed on through generations," said Ryder.

"I like that. But why are there so many gifts under the tree?" asked Piper.

"It's one of many ways people show love," said Sienna. "Gifts are a way of saying it's better to give than to receive."

"Will there be a gift for me under the tree?" Piper inquired.

Ryder laughed. "Of course, the family loves you. Last year I wanted a ball, but I got you instead."

Piper gave a big, goofy grin and said, "Best gift ever!"

"You're right," Ryder replied.

Sienna thought about how far Ryder and Piper had come as siblings this year. She had heard them play, fight, ignore, teach, laugh, love, and so much more. There had been times when she wanted to bop them each on the head for being so stubborn. But there were also times when she wished they could see just how good they had been for each other. Regardless, she had not envied them in any way.

Ryder had been lonely for the companionship of another dog—even if he hadn't realized it. Piper brought him out of his shell. Though Ryder was still shy, he did laugh more, and he learned to compromise and teach with patience.

The things Piper learned were countless. The older she got, the more she understood right from wrong. Though she wasn't one to admit when she was wrong, Ryder did teach her how to do it gracefully.

She also had learned that putting others before herself was essential. As much as she liked to be on the go, she'd also realized the value of what could be done by just being still. Ryder had taught her love, loyalty, and companionship.

Sienna admired the two dogs but did not envy the past year. She secretly hoped that she'd played a small part in refereeing the battles.

And so, the family gathered for a traditional Christmas Eve dinner and stood side-by-side for the family photo. Everyone wore Pjs, including Ryder and Piper.

When Piper saw Ryder dressed in red- and green-stripped pajamas with a hood that had pointed elf ears, she howled with laughter. "You look like one of Santa's helpers! I'm going to bite you in the butt if you come down the chimney!"

Ryder smirked. "You're next," he said. "Let's see how you feel in this ridiculous outfit."

Piper didn't care; she wanted to be dressed like the rest of the family. She happily ran to Mom and stood quietly while the pajama was pulled up to her head, which now had pointed elf ears. She and Ryder looked like twins.

With big smiles, the family posed and waited for the camera to click.

"Finally, it's done!" said Ryder.

"We have to do it again," said Piper. "Sienna isn't wearing Pjs."

"Sienna doesn't wear pajamas," Ryder said mockingly.

Sienna quickly answered, "That's because I'm special," she said.

On Christmas day, the family gathered around the tree. They were all excited about opening gifts, but no one was more excited than Piper. She waited patiently, watching Sienna joyfully swish her paw at ribbons and bows on the floor.

When Sienna saw Piper watching her, she pushed a piece of wrapping paper in her direction.

"Go ahead," she said. "Give it a try. You'll slide across the floor."

Piper dashed across the room and jumped onto the paper. She swished her paws, trying to make it slide. But the paper didn't move. Instead, she tripped and fell, landing flat on her stomach. "That wasn't fun at all," she mumbled.

"Well, it is for me!" Sienna said as she took off and slid about two feet on the same piece of paper.

Piper wasn't impressed. She sat beside Ryder and asked him what he wanted for Christmas.

"I want a ball. You keep chewing holes in the ones we have and then they don't bounce. I want a ball that will bounce. What about you? What would you like?"

"I would like a bone to chew on for hours," replied Piper.

"I hope you get one, so you don't chew my new ball."

"Ryder, are you sorry you got me instead of a ball for Christmas last year?" Piper asked.

"Piper, I'll be honest. I was upset, but I've come to see that you're more fun than a ball. And, even though you drive me nuts sometimes, we do have fun. We may not always agree but that's okay. I've never *loved* a ball or had one love me back. But, I do love you. You're the best gift I could have ever received."

Piper jumped on her brother. "I love you too. I guess we could say that you were my first Christmas gift!"

Finally, Mom picked up a gift bag from under the Christmas tree. She called Ryder over and he immediately came and sat at her feet. She opened the bag for him and pulled out a new blue and orange ball. "Merry Christmas, you are such a good boy," she said.

Ryder wiggled his short, nubby tail. Mom held out the ball, and he gently took it with his mouth. He went over to his bed and happily started rolling it back and forth with his nose. He waited patiently, waiting for someone to take him outside to throw the ball across the lawn.

Mom called Piper, and she zoomed across the room. Her entire body shook from her tail to her head. The family was laughing at how excited Piper was to receive a gift. The more laughter, the harder Piper wagged.

Mom opened Piper's bag and pulled out a bone, "Piper, here is something you're allowed to chew on. Enjoy, little girl. Merry Christmas."

Piper grabbed the bone as fast as she could while being careful not to touch Mom with her teeth. She took the bone over to Ryder and dropped it on the floor.

"Very nice," said Ryder.

Piper showed the bone to Sienna. "Is it your turn to receive a gift?

"I'm happy with ribbons and wrapping paper," said Sienna haughtily. "I don't need anything else!"

Mom went over to the tree, picked up a wicker basket, and placed it on the floor for everyone to see. "Sienna!" she called. "It's your turn for a gift."

Ryder and Piper walked over to the basket, but Sienna backed away.

"Sienna!" called Mom. "Your gift is inside this basket."

When the basket lid popped open, Ryder and Piper looked inside. At first, they giggled and then chuckled. And finally, they laughed so hard that they fell on top of each other.

Sienna wondered what was so funny, so she cautiously approached the basket but didn't look inside.

"There's no need to fret," said Mom. "We got you a little brother."

Sienna peeked into the basket, hoping to see a baby boy who looked like Mother and Father. What she saw was shocking. A ball of black fur with whiskers and a tail looked up at her and meowed softly.

"Oh, dear," said Sienna sadly. "It's a—a kitten!"

Holding back more laughter, Ryder and Piper walked away.

"Oh, my," said Ryder. "From here on in, I'm sure all our lives are going to be interesting."

And so, new adventures and a lot of fun were ahead for all the animals on Southern Seasons Farm.

ABOUT THE AUTHOR

Kathy Duffy and her husband live on Southern Seasons Farm, in Georgia. They have two adult daughters and over 20 animals. Kathy began reading to her daughters at an early age and believes it contributed to their love of books. She also believes that children should be allowed to read what makes them happy even if the topic is redundant.

"Whatever topic gets a book in their hands, is what they should read about. If that means twenty books in a row about horses, so be it."

Many of the animals on her farm are rescued because she roots for the underdog and will adopt the ones many people turn down.

Kathy is planning to dedicate each of the books in the Tails from Southern Seasons Farm series to different animal rescue group along with a portion of the proceeds.